MOLLY AND THE LOCKDOWN

For health and care workers everywhere.

Molly and the Lockdown published by Graffeg in 2021.
Copyright © Graffeg Limited 2021.

ISBN 9781914079399

Text © Malachy Doyle, illustrations © Andrew Whitson,
design and production Graffeg Limited. This publication
and content is protected by copyright © 2021.

Malachy Doyle and Andrew Whitson are hereby identified
as the authors of this work in accordance with section 77 of
the Copyrights, Designs and Patents Act 1988.

A CIP Catalogue record for this book is available from the
British Library.

Mali a'r Cyfnod Clo (Welsh edition) ISBN 9781914079405
Muireann agus an Dianghlasáil (Irish edition)
ISBN 9781912929122

Teaching Resources
www.graffeg.com/pages/teachers-resources

1 2 3 4 5 6 7 8 9

THIS BOOK BELONGS TO

_____

_____

_____

_____

MALACHY DOYLE ANDREW WHITSON

MOLLY AND THE LOCKDOWN

GRAFFEG

'The island's locked down! The island's locked down!'

Dylan was running around like a mad thing, yelling his head off.

'What are you on about, boy?' asked Molly.

'Nobody's allowed on or off because of this really bad flu thing that's going about!' he told her.

'Mum, Mum, what'll happen to Dad now the island's locked down?' cried Molly, when she got home.

Her father was over on the mainland, selling fish.

'I'm afraid he might have to stay there for now, love,' said her mother. 'It'll be hard for us, but we have to keep the island safe. I'm sure it won't be for long.'

But even a week's a long time when you're missing your lovely dad...

'I want you to help your mother around the place,' he told Molly, over the phone. 'I'll be back just as soon as I can.'

'But I'm worried you'll get sick, Dad. They say lots of people are getting sick.'

'I'll be fine here at Uncle Ed's house,' replied her father. 'We're keeping away from people as much as possible, and wearing face masks if we have to go out.'

So Molly helped with the cooking. She helped with the ducks and the chickens.

Her mother asked her to help make some masks for their fellow-islanders...

'But why, Mum?' asked Molly. 'Nobody's sick here.'

'Yes, but it's better to be safe than sorry,' said her mum. 'Let's hope we don't need them.'

Although the lockdown went on a lot longer than a week, life wasn't all that different for Molly, apart from her dad being away.

But one morning, when she popped round with a fish pie for Mary Kate, the old woman was having a bad turn.

'Run and fetch Nurse Ellen, there's a good girl,' she gasped, from her bed.

So Molly ran – and when Nurse Ellen came, she said Mary Kate had to go to hospital.

'Is it the flu? The really bad flu?' Molly whispered to her mum, who'd come over to help.

'No, love,' said her mum. 'It's her heart.'

'But how will she get to hospital?' asked Molly. 'Nobody's allowed off the island!'

'I know,' said her mum. 'But she badly needs a doctor. We've no choice.'

15

So Nurse Ellen called up the lifeboat.

She made a few special requests too, so the lifeboat men brought toffees and toilet paper, and all the things that the island was in danger of running out of.

And then they took Mary Kate off to hospital.

But somehow, though everyone had been extra-specially careful, the lifeboat must have brought something else to the island. Something bad...

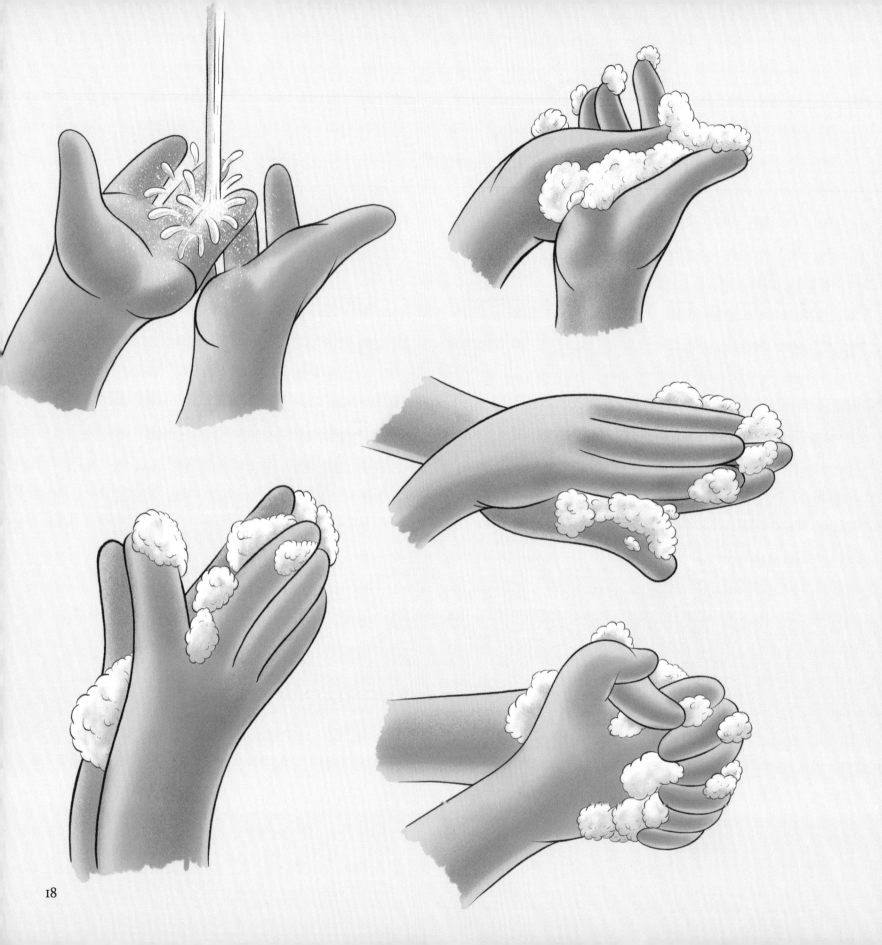

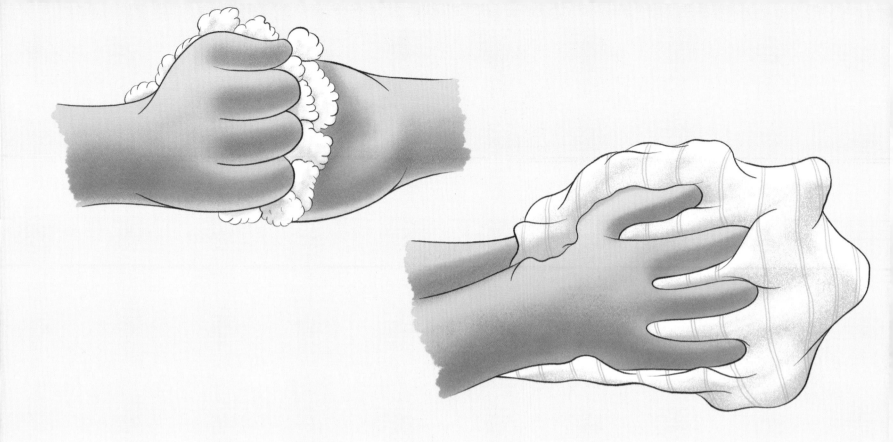

Two weeks later, the school had closed down and everyone was asked to stay at home.

The virus had reached the island and they all had to try and stop it spreading – by washing their hands lots and lots, and by wearing masks if they really needed to go out.

Only Nurse Ellen was allowed to visit people.

Oh, and Molly's mum, who'd offered to help her.

So Molly had to do most of the jobs around the house, all by herself.

She let the dog out, when he needed a wee...

She called in the chickens to feed them – and then she decided it'd be easier to just keep them in the back room...

She did the cooking and cleaning, and made a load more masks all by herself, because her mum was dashing round the island, helping people...

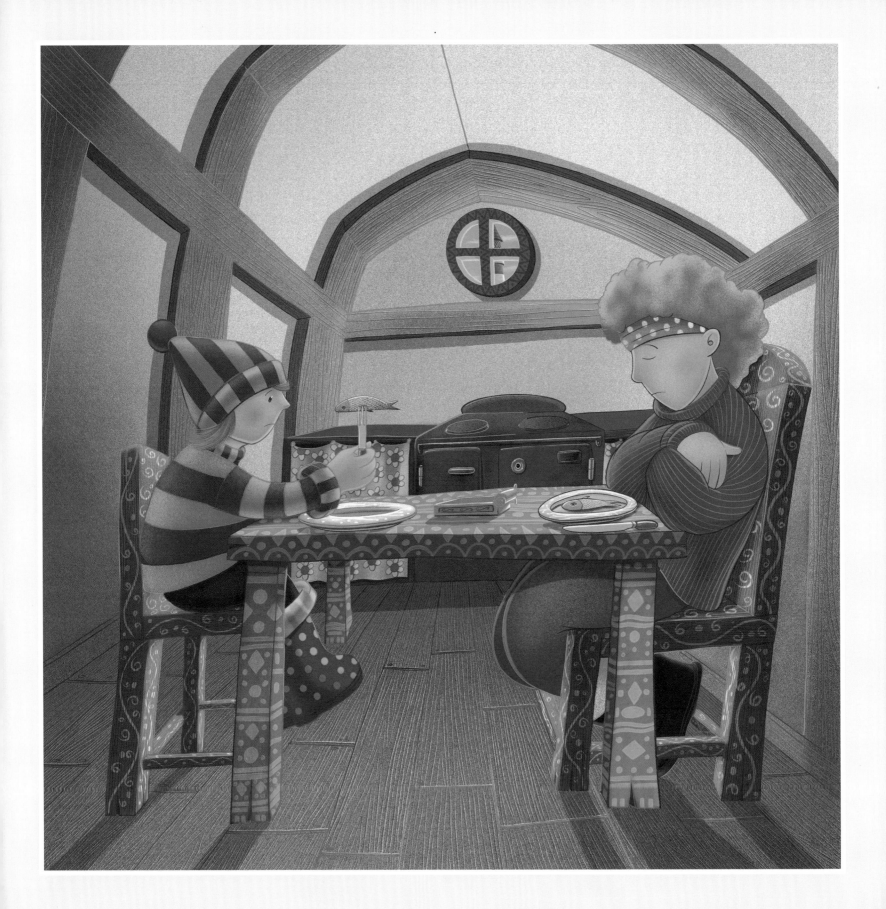

Three weeks later, Molly and her mum were down to eating tinned sardines – and for a family of fisherfolk, that means things were pretty bad.

Four more islanders had been taken to hospital by then, while others were ill at home.

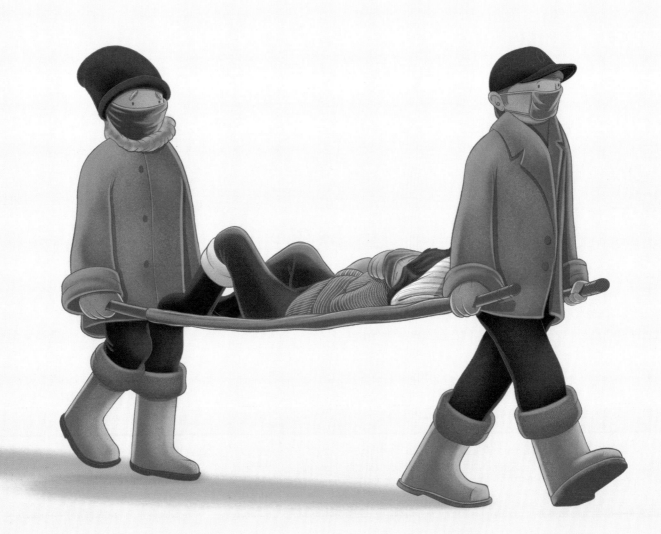

The lockdown went on for a long time.
A long, long time.

Molly was missing school, she was missing her friends, but most of all...

'How are you doing, Dad?' she said, over the phone. 'I miss you so much.'

'I miss you too, love – you and Mum,' said her father. 'And Uncle Ed here's driving me mad. He stomps around the house all day, bellowing away on the bagpipes!'

Molly did all her schoolwork. She taught the dog tricks, and they did keep fit together.

She did all her jigsaws in world record time, and talked to Dylan and her friends on the phone.

She read her favourite books, over and over, and enjoyed some new ones too.

She spoke to her teacher and, as often as possible, to her lovely dad – when she could hear him over the noise of Uncle Ed's bagpipes!

And do you know what? In time, the lockdown eased.

Even Mary Kate returned, safe and well.

And while not everything got back to normal straight away, in a funny way Molly quite enjoyed having so much time at home, just her and the dog and the ducks and the chickens...

She even got a bit better on the fiddle.

But it was so good to get back to school, once it re-opened.

It was brilliant to be back with her friends, even if they still had to keep a little distance from each other.

And at last, at long last, they were told there was a new way to protect everyone – a way to stop people getting the virus...

It would mean a big needle in your arm, and who likes big needles? But it'd be worth it. It would definitely be worth it.

'More good news, Moll…' said her father, later. 'I'll be home in the morning. Is there anything you want, love?'

'Only you, Dad,' said Molly. 'Only you, safe and well.'

All the islanders were down at the harbour to welcome Molly's father back.

And the first person to greet him as he stepped off the boat was... you guessed it... Molly.

'That jab had better work, so there's no more lockdowns!' she yelled, up on her daddy's shoulders.

'I don't think there will be, love,' said Molly's mum. 'But if there are, Thomas,' she added, with a smile, 'make sure you're not on the mainland.'

'And put up with Uncle Ed on the bagpipes one second longer?' said Molly's dad, with a laugh. 'No chance!'

Malachy Doyle

Malachy Doyle grew up by the sea in Northern Ireland, and after living in Wales for many years has returned to Ireland. He and his wife Liz bought an old farmhouse on a small island off the coast of Donegal, where they live with their dogs, cats and ducks.

Malachy has had well over a hundred books published, from pop-up books for toddlers to gritty teenage novels. Over the years he has won many prestigious book awards, and his work is available in around thirty languages.

As well as the three previous stories in the Molly series, *Molly and the Stormy Sea, Molly and the Whale* and *Molly and the Lighthouse,* his recent books include *The Miracle of Hanukkah, Rama and Sita, Jack and the Jungle* and *Big Bad Biteasaurus* (Bloomsbury), *Fug and the Thumps* (Firefly Press), *Cinderfella* (Walker Books) and *Ootch Cootch* (Graffeg), which is illustrated by his daughter, Hannah Doyle.

Andrew Whitson

Andrew Whitson is an award-winning artist and Belfast native who likes to be called Mr. Ando! He lives in an old house which is nestled discreetly on the side of a misty hill; at the edge of a magic wood, below an enchanted castle in the shadow of a giant's nose. His house looks down over Belfast Harbour where the Titanic was built and up at the Belfast Cavehill where an American B-17 Flying Fortress bomber plane once crashed during World War II!

Mr. Ando makes pictures for books in the tower of a very old church and works so late that he often gets locked in. He has therefore forged a secret magic key which he keeps at his side at all times and uses to escape from the church when there is no one else around.

Mr. Ando has illustrated over twenty books under his own name, the most recent of which being the *Molly* series with Malachy Doyle and the award winning *Rita* series of picture books with Myra Zepf.